A Note to Parents and Caregivers:

With a focus on math, science, and social studies, *Read-it!* Readers support both the learning of content information and the extension of more complex reading skills. They encourage the development of problem-solving skills that help children expand their thinking.

 The PURPLE LEVEL presents basic topics and objects using high frequency words and simple language patterns.

 The RED LEVEL presents familiar topics using common words and repeating sentence patterns.

 The BLUE LEVEL presents new ideas using a larger vocabulary and varied sentence structure.

 The YELLOW LEVEL presents more challenging ideas, a broad vocabulary, and wide variety in sentence structure.

 The GREEN LEVEL presents more complex ideas, an extended vocabulary range, and expanded language structures.

 The ORANGE LEVEL presents a wide range of ideas and concepts using challenging vocabulary and complex language structures.

When sharing a content focused book with your child, read to find out facts and concepts, pausing often to restate and talk about the new information. The realistic story format provides an opportunity to talk about the language used, and to learn about reading to problem-solve for information. Encourage children to measure, make maps, and consider other situations that allow them to apply what they are learning.

There is no right or wrong way to share books with children. Find time to read and share new learning with your child, and pass on the legacy of literacy.

Adria F. Klein, Ph.D.
Professor Emeritus
California State University
San Bernardino, California

Editor: Shelly Lyons
Designer: Tracy Davies
Page Production: Melissa Kes
Art Director: Nathan Gassman
Associate Managing Editor: Christianne Jones
The illustrations in this book were created digitally.

Picture Window Books
5115 Excelsior Boulevard
Suite 232
Minneapolis, MN 55416
877-845-8392
www.picturewindowbooks.com

Printed in the United States of America.

 All books published by Picture Window Books
are manufactured with paper containing at least
10 percent post-consumer waste.

Library of Congress Cataloging-in-Publication Data
Blaisdell, Molly, 1964-
The grass patch project / by Molly Blaisdell ; illustrated by James Demski, Jr.
p. cm. — (Read-it! readers: Science)
ISBN-13: 978-1-4048-2292-4 (library binding)
ISBN-10: 1-4048-2292-5 (library binding)
1. Grasses—Juvenile literature. 2. Botany projects—Juvenile literature.
I. Demski, James, 1976- ill. II. Title.
QK495.G74.B58 2008
584'.9—dc22   2007004572

The Grass Patch Project

by Molly Blaisdell
illustrated by James Demski Jr.

Special thanks to our advisers for their expertise:

Mary Meyer, Ph.D.
Professor and Extension Horticulturist
University of Minnesota, Department of Horticultural Science
Minnesota Landscape Arboretum, Chaska, Minnesota

Adria F. Klein, Ph.D.
Professor Emeritus, California State University
San Bernardino, California

PICTURE WINDOW BOOKS
Minneapolis, Minnesota

Jason looked at his new school. His old school had been in the country. Huge fields of grass had grown around it. No grass grew near his new school in the city. He missed seeing those fields. He was still wishing for green grass when the bell rang. He hurried to his classroom.

Jason sat at his desk. This was his second day at Sunrise Elementary. Everything was still new. But today it was time to get to work.

"Our Earth Day project is eight weeks away," his teacher, Mrs. McVey, said.

Emily raised her hand. She asked, "What's Earth Day?"

5

"Earth Day is on April 22," said Mrs. McVey. "We have a party for our planet. All of the classes do something that helps Earth."

"What kinds of things?" Emily asked.

"Recycling, cleanup, tree planting, or anything that helps Earth," said Mrs. McVey. "There are prizes for the best projects. Does anyone have any ideas for our class project?"

Jason raised his hand. It was his turn to speak up. "I do," he said.

"What's your idea?" Mrs. McVey asked.

"We could plant grass," Jason said. "My old school had lots of grass around it. I saw a great place in front of this school where we could plant grass."

Grass is a kind of plant with thin leaves called blades. There are many different kinds of grass. Some examples are Kentucky bluegrass, Bermuda, and fescue.

Emily raised her hand. "We could plant a tree," she said.

"Everyone will do that," Ray said. "I think we should pick up trash. That would really help Earth. How would grass help our planet?"

"That's a good question," Mrs. McVey said.

Jason knew growing grass was a good idea. His hand shot up.

"Grass is a plant," he said. "Plants make clean air for us."

Green plants make a gas called oxygen through a process called photosynthesis. During photosynthesis, plant leaves take in sunlight, a gas called carbon dioxide, and water to make food and oxygen. Humans and other animals need oxygen to live.

"Are there other ways grass might help our planet?" Mrs. McVey asked.

"When it rains, water washes soil onto our sidewalks," Emily said. "Grass would keep the soil in place."

Wind and water wear away soil. The wearing away is called erosion. Grass roots hold the soil together. The roots stop the soil from wearing away. On mountains, in swamps, and in deserts, grass roots keep soil in place.

"Any more thoughts?" Mrs. McVey asked.

"Some farm animals eat grass," Jamal said.
"Grass is food."

A · B · C · D · E · F

EARTH DAY PROJECT IDEAS
- PLANT A TREE
- PICK UP TRASH
PLANT GRASS

Jamal and Emily were in charge of spreading the compost. All of the kids in the class helped mix it in to the soil.

Next, they smoothed the area with rakes.

Ray was in charge of spreading the grass seed. It was the biggest job. Ray sprinkled the seeds evenly on the soil. Everyone used rakes to softly mix the soil and seeds together. Ray said mixing the seeds into the soil would help keep them from blowing away in the wind.

"OK, everyone," Jason said. "Get your watering cans ready."

The class watered the patch until the soil was damp, not muddy.

Twice a day, the class had to water the grass patch. It was important for the soil to be wet for the grass to grow.

On the fourth day, Ray spoke up.

"Where is the grass?" he asked. "We aren't going to win the prize."

"The grass will grow," Jason said. "Just wait." Jason tried to sound sure. But he wasn't sure.

The next day, there still wasn't any grass.
"Where is the grass?" asked Jamal.
Jason stared at his shoes.

Mrs. McVey said, "It could be another week before the first blades of grass pop up. Let's give the grass some more time."

After planting, a grass seed starts growing beneath the soil. First, the outer layer, or seed coat, opens. Next, the grass roots grow downward. Then, the grass shoot pushes its way upward through the soil and becomes a blade.

The next week, Jason went to check on the grass patch.

He saw green fuzz instead of just soil. Shoots of grass had come up! Everyone was happy.

Six weeks after spreading the grass seed, the class checked their grass patch. The grass was two inches high.

"You had a great idea," Ray said.

Later that day, it was time to choose the winners of the school's Earth Day contest.

"Tell us about your project," one judge said.

"We grew a grass patch," said Jason.

26

"Grass makes our school beautiful," Emily said.

"Grass is strong, too," Jamal said. "Kids can run and play on it!"

The class waited for the judges to vote. Ray
went up to Jason.

"I wasn't sure the grass would really grow,"
Ray said.

"I know," Jason said.

"But it did grow, and I had fun," Ray said. "Even if we don't win, I think your idea was the best one."

"Thanks," Jason said. He liked growing the grass patch. But he liked making a new friend even more.

At the end of the day, the judges announced the winners of the contest.

"Mrs. McVey's class wins for their Grass Patch Project," said one judge.

All of the kids jumped up and down.

Jason and Ray jumped the highest.

Activity: Growing Grass

Items needed:
- a ½-pint (.2-liter) sized milk carton
- a spray bottle full of water
- grass seed
- potting mix
- a bowl
- a ruler

Directions:
1. Ask an adult to punch small holes in the bottom of an empty milk carton.
2. Open the top of the carton and fill it with potting mix. Place it in a bowl to catch water.
3. Sprinkle grass seed on top.
4. Cover the seeds with a small amount of potting mix.
5. Spray the mix twice a day with water from the spray bottle.
6. Keep the carton in a sunny spot. Wait several days for grass to appear.

Glossary
blade—a grass leaf
compost—a mix that may include rotting leaves, grass, manure, and vegetables
erosion—to wear away Earth's surface with wind and water
leaves—the flat, green parts of a plant that grow from the stem
manure—the waste matter of animals like cows or chickens
minerals—tiny bits of non-living material that help plants grow
photosynthesis—a process plants use to make food and oxygen
root—the part of a plant that grows down into the ground and takes in water and minerals to feed the plant
seed—the part of a flowering plant from which a new plant will grow
seed coat—the outer layer of the seed
shoot—a bit of new growth
soil—another word for dirt

Life Cycle of Grass

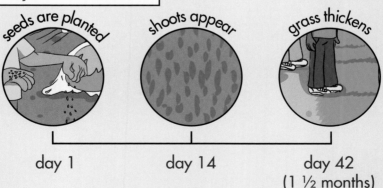

seeds are planted

shoots appear

grass thickens

day 1

day 14

day 42
(1 ½ months)

31

To Learn More

At the Library

Koontz, Robin. *Composting: Nature's Recyclers*. Minneapolis: Picture Window Books, 2007.

Loves, June. *Grass*. Philadelphia: Chelsea ClubHouse, 2005.

Mattern, Joanne. *How Grass Grows*. Milwaukee: Weekly Reader Early Learning Library, 2006.

On the Web

FactHound offers a safe, fun way to find Web sites related to this book. All of the sites on FactHound have been researched by our staff.

1. Visit *www.facthound.com*
2. Type in this special code: 1404822925
3. Click on the FETCH IT button.

Your trusty FactHound will fetch the best sites for you!

Look for all of the books in the *Read-it!* Readers: Science series:

Friends and Flowers (life science: bulbs)
The Grass Patch Project (life science: grass)
The Sunflower Farmer (life science: sunflowers)
Surprising Beans (life science: beans)